The Boy Who Ate

Ate

Christmas

Chris Duke

For Colin & Jill in their forever year 2024.

"Lots of people want to ride with you in the limo, but a true friend is someone who will take the bus with you when the limo breaks down."

Chapters

Chapter 1: Magic on Every Street

In the sweet little town of Christmas Presence, every day was like December 25th. The streets were always strung with twinkling fairy lights, the air completely filled with the jingle of sleigh bells, and the smell of mince pies wafted from every open window. It was a town where snowmen stood all year round, their carrot noses defiantly ignoring the seasons.

In this everlasting winter wonderland lived a boy named Teddy Tumshie. Now, Teddy wasn't your ordinary, run-of-the-mill child. He had a reputation, one that wasn't exactly glowing. Teddy was known far and wide, from the top of the Christmas tree in the town square to the bottom of the deepest snowdrift, for being particularly selfish and his never ending greed—especially when it came to Christmas treats.

Teddy wasn't just fond of Christmas sweets but obsessed with them. His eyes twinkled not with festive joy but with the reflection of sugar plums and candy canes. His room was a treasure trove of pilfered pudding, covert cookies, and secret stashes of stolen sweets. If there was a mince pie missing from a windowsill, a chocolate Santa unaccounted for, or a mysterious disappearance of Mrs Figgy's famous fruitcake, you could bet your last candy cane that Teddy Tumshie was behind it.

But it wasn't just his sweet tooth that made Teddy infamous. No, it was his lack of sharing. He never offered anyone a biscuit or a slice of cake, not even his best friend, Timmy Tinsel, who was as skinny as a candy cane and twice as sweet.

On this particularly frosty morning, the sun shone, the birds were carolling (as they do in Christmas Presence), and Teddy was up to his usual shenanigans. He had just spotted Mrs Jingle's freshly baked gingerbread men cooling on her windowsill. Licking his lips with a mischievous glint in his eye, Teddy tiptoed towards the prize.

Just as he was about to swipe a gingerbread man, or five, he heard a voice, "Teddy Tumshie! What do you think you're doing?"

Startled, Teddy spun around. It was his grandmother, Granny Tumshie, her hands firmly planted on her hips. She had that look in her eye—the one that said, 'I know exactly what you're up to, young man.'

"Nothing, Granny," Teddy replied, trying his best to look innocent, a feat quite tricky when your hand is hovering suspiciously close to a tray of gingerbread men.

Granny Tumshie raised an eyebrow. "Well, if you're doing nothing, you can help me in the attic. I need to fetch the Christmas decorations down. It's almost time for the annual Christmas Presence festival, and we're behind schedule!"

Teddy groaned. The attic was dusty, musty, and full of forgotten things—definitely not as appealing as Mrs. Jingle's gingerbread men. But he knew better than to argue with Granny Tumshie.

As they climbed up the creaky ladder into the attic, little did Teddy know that he was about to stumble upon something extraordinary, something that would change Christmas Presence forever. And it wasn't just another hidden stash of sweets...

Chapter 2: Secrets in the Shadows

The attic of the Tumshie household was a strange and wondrous place. It was like a museum of Christmases past, brimming with tinsel-covered memories and dust-layered decorations. Teddy, however, wasn't interested in nostalgia. He was more concerned about spiderwebs and possibly encountering a Christmas ghost.

As Granny Tumshie rummaged through boxes labelled 'Xmas 1922' and 'Fragile: Glass Baubles,' Teddy's eyes wandered. That's when he saw it—an old, cobweb-covered gingerbread house tucked away in the corner. It wasn't just any gingerbread house. This one seemed to sparkle with ancient magic, its icing shimmering in the dim light of the attic.

"Granny, what's this?" Teddy asked, his curiosity momentarily overshadowing his greed.

Granny Tumshie turned, her eyes widening slightly as she saw what Teddy had found. "Oh, that old thing? It's been in our family for generations. Legend believes it's a magical gingerbread house, but it's just a silly old tale. Best leave it be, Teddy."

But Teddy wasn't listening. His mind was racing with the thought of having an entire gingerbread house all to himself. His greedy little heart thumped with excitement. Magical or not, it was the largest piece of Christmas confectionery he'd ever seen!

Ignoring Granny's warnings, he waited until she was distracted by a box of twinkling fairy lights. With a quick glance to ensure he wasn't being watched, Teddy carefully lifted the gingerbread house. It was heavier than he expected, and he nearly dropped it twice on his way down the attic ladder.

Once in the safety of his room, Teddy marvelled at his prize. The gumdrop decorations, the candy cane doorposts, the icing-covered roof – it was magnificent. And yet, there was something about it that made Teddy pause. It almost seemed to be... whispering?

"Don't be daft, Teddy," he told himself. "It's just a gingerbread house, not a talking one!"

That night, as Teddy lay in bed, the gingerbread house on his dresser, he couldn't shake off a feeling of unease. There was something about the house that was more than meets the eye. But his greed blinded him to the warning bells ringing in his head.

In the silent hours of the night, a faint glow began to seep from the gingerbread house. Its magic was awakening; with it, a change was about to sweep over Christmas Presence. A change that Teddy, in his greed, had unwittingly unleashed.

Little did he know that his actions would have consequences far beyond a stomach ache from too many sweets. The magic of Christmas was delicate, and Teddy had just tipped the first domino in a chain of events that could end Christmas Presence's festive cheer forever.

Chapter 3: The Fading of Festive Lights

Teddy Tumshie's morning began like any other in Christmas Presence, except this time, he awoke with a newfound treasure—the gingerbread house. The allure of the candy-coated roof and icing-adorned walls was too tempting to resist. Teddy broke off a shard of the sugary roof without hesitation and popped it into his mouth. The taste was divine, a symphony of sweetness that danced on his tongue.

As he indulged, something strange started to unfold outside. Christmas Presence's once vibrant and twinkling Christmas lights began to dim, like stars fading in the dawn sky. The garlands, usually so lush and green, seemed to droop sadly. The whole town was slowly but surely losing its Christmas cheer.

Down on Jolly Avenue, Mrs. Jingle, known for her award-winning Christmas light display, was in a tizzy. "My lights! My beautiful twinkling lights! They're not twinkling anymore!" she cried, frantically adjusting the bulbs. Her neighbours gathered, equally concerned at the dull display.

Meanwhile, the giant Christmas tree, usually a beacon of joy and festivity, stood less grand at the town square. Its lights flickered weakly, the vibrant reds and greens of the baubles now dull and washed out. The townsfolk gathering around the square felt an unusual chill, not of the cold but of a dwindling spirit.

Even the local café's steaming hot chocolate and freshly baked Christmas cookies failed to lift the residents' spirits. The usual hum of cheerful conversation was replaced by murmurs of confusion and concern. "What's happening to our town?" they whispered, sipping their lukewarm drinks.

Back in Teddy's room, he continued his feast on the magical gingerbread house, unaware of the chaos unfolding. With every piece he ate, the enchantment that bound the spirit of Christmas to the town weakened. The once glowing house was now looking as hopeless as the town itself.

Teddy, however, was too engrossed in his sugary plunder to notice the link. His thoughts were only of the next piece to devour, his eyes gleaming with greed and delight. He had already eaten his way through half of the gingerbread walls, his stomach beginning to protest, but his desire for more overpowering his sense of fullness.

As the day progressed, the festive atmosphere in Christmas Presence continued to wane. Carolers on street corners tried to lift the spirits with their songs, but their voices lacked warmth and feeling. Shoppers moved through the stores with lifeless steps, their holiday enthusiasm seemingly drained away.

Mr. Sprinklesworth, the town's beloved baker, noticed the change too. His bakery, always filled with the aroma of cinnamon and nutmeg, now seemed to lack its usual zest. "It's as if the flavour of Christmas is fading," he mused, puzzled by the boring taste of his famous Christmas cupcakes.

By nightfall, the changes were undeniable. The star atop the Christmas tree in the square barely glowed, the festive window displays in shops were dim and uninviting, and a sense of gloom had settled over Christmas Presence.

In his room, surrounded by the leftovers of the gingerbread house, Teddy finally paused. For the first time, he looked out his window at the town he had always known to be vibrant and lively, now shadowed and muted. A twinge of unease crept into his heart, but he quickly shook it off, reaching for another piece of the gingerbread house.

As he took the last bite, finishing off the final corner of the once-magical creation, the last bit of sparkle vanished from the town. The connection was clear, but Teddy, with his belly full of gingerbread and a heart not yet open to understanding, failed to see it. He had unwittingly dimmed the light of Christmas Presence, and the consequences of his greed were just beginning to unfold.

Chapter 4: Mysteries of Mr. Sprinklesworth

Teddy Tumshie, his stomach full but his heart strangely empty, decided to take a stroll through Christmas Presence. As he walked, he couldn't help but notice the stark changes around him. The once vibrant tinsel looked tarnished, the merry wreaths hung limply, and the carolers' songs sounded more like melancholic melodies than joyous jingles.

"What's happened to this place?" Teddy muttered to himself, feeling a puzzling sense of unease. He couldn't quite understand why the town seemed so different. It was as if someone had turned down the dial on Christmas itself.

A familiar scent tickled his nose as he wandered through the streets. This scent reminded him of the gingerbread house. Following the aroma like a detective on the trail, Teddy stood outside Mr Sprinklesworth's bakery, the most beloved in all of Christmas Presence.

Pushing open the door, he was greeted by the warm, comforting smell of gingerbread and smoke from the unusually loud coal baking oven. It was bustling inside, but not with the usual cheerfulness. The townsfolk were there, whispering worriedly among themselves, their expressions reflecting the gloom upon the town.

Mr. Sprinklesworth, a jolly man who usually wore a constant smile under his flour-dusted moustache, now looked solemn. He pulled a tray of gingerbread cookies out of the oven when he noticed Teddy.

"Ah, Teddy! Just the lad I wanted to see," said Mr. Sprinklesworth, his tone serious.

Teddy, feeling a flutter of nerves, approached the counter. "Is something wrong, Mr. Sprinklesworth?"

The baker leaned in, his voice low. "Teddy, have you noticed anything... unusual happening in town?"

Teddy nodded, still not making the connection with his own actions.

Mr. Sprinklesworth sighed deeply. "I believe it has something to do with an ancient gingerbread house. A magical one, tied to the very heart of Christmas Presence."

Teddy's heart skipped a beat. The gingerbread house? How could Mr. Sprinklesworth possibly know about that?

Seeing the confusion on Teddy's face, the baker continued, "This gingerbread house, it's not just a confection, Teddy. It's a symbol of our town's spirit, its joy, and its love for Christmas. Legend says that

Christmas Presence will flourish in endless cheer as long as the house remains intact. But if it were ever to be... consumed, the town would lose its Christmas spirit."

Teddy felt a cold shiver run down his spine. He thought of the now almost wholly eaten gingerbread house hidden in his room. Could it be the same one?

Mr. Sprinklesworth, mistaking Teddy's silence for confusion, placed a comforting hand on his shoulder. "I know it sounds like a fairy tale, but look around, Teddy. The town is losing its cheer, and I fear it's because the gingerbread house is in danger."

Teddy's mind raced. He wanted to confess, to tell Mr. Sprinklesworth everything, but his words were stuck in his throat. The realisation of what he had done was overwhelming. His greed, his selfishness, had harmed the entire town.

"Thank you, Mr. Sprinklesworth," Teddy managed to say, his voice barely a whisper. He left the bakery quickly, his mind in turmoil.

As he walked back through the dreary streets of Christmas Presence, Teddy knew he had to make things right. But how? The gingerbread house was nearly gone, with it, the town's Christmas spirit. He needed a plan and fast.

His actions weighed heavily on him, a burden far heavier than any amount of stolen sweets. For the first time, Teddy Tumshie felt something he had never truly felt before...regret.

Chapter 5: The Dimming of Christmas Presence

In the heart of Christmas Presence, a transformation was underway, but not the kind anyone wished for. The once joyous town, known for its year-round festive spirit, was now cloaked in an air of gloom. The changes were subtle at first, but they became impossible to ignore as the days passed.

The carolers, who once sang with voices bright and full of cheer, now gathered in the town square with gloomy tunes and melodies that echoed the town's growing sorrow. "Silent Night" had never sounded so literal and mournful.

Even the snow, which typically blanketed the town in a pristine white, seemed to have lost its lustre. It fell in listless flurries, painting the town in shades of dull grey rather than sparkling white. Children who usually played boisterously in the snow now trudged through it sluggishly, their laughter and joy a distant memory.

Once a vibrant display of Christmas merriment, shop windows now reflected the town's sorrowful mood. Mannequins dressed in festive attire seemed to droop, their colours faded, and the twinkling lights that framed the displays were dim and lifeless.

Perhaps the most telling sign of the town's plight was Mrs. Jingle, the embodiment of Christmas spirit in Christmas Presence. Known for her bright red coats and jolly laughter, she now wandered the streets in a plain grey shawl, her smile a rare sight. In a symbolic gesture that shocked the townsfolk, she officially changed her name to Mrs. Meh. The news spread like a cold winter chill, dampening the spirits of everyone who heard it.

"Christmas is just not the same this year," Mrs. Meh said to anyone who asked, her voice missing its usual warmth. "I don't feel like a 'Jingle' anymore. 'Meh' is what this holiday has become."

The town's famous Christmas market, a hub of activity and cheer, now had half-empty stalls. Vendors who usually sold handcrafted ornaments and festive treats now stood behind their booths with half-hearted attempts to attract customers. Once so inviting, the scent of mulled wine and roasted chestnuts now barely wafted through the air.

At the heart of the town, the grand Christmas tree, which usually stood tall and proud, was now a sad sight. Its lights flickered weakly, the star at its top no longer shining. The presents that lay beneath it, once a mountain of colourful boxes, were now a tiny gathering of drab, poorly wrapped gifts.

Even the animals of Christmas Presence felt the change. Usually spirited and playful, the reindeer in the local farm now huddled together, their eyes lacking their usual sparkle. The birds, which typically filled the air with merry chirping, were silent as if they also mourned the loss of Christmas cheer.

As Teddy Tumshie walked through the streets, witnessing the impact of his actions, his heart sank. The joy and vibrancy that had once defined Christmas Presence faded everywhere he looked. He realised that the gingerbread house was more than just a treat; it was the heart of the town's Christmas spirit.

Filled with a growing sense of responsibility, Teddy knew he had to find a way to bring back the Christmas cheer to Christmas Presence. But how could he restore something he had so carelessly consumed? The answer escaped him, but he knew he couldn't give up. Christmas Presence depended on it.

Chapter 6: Teddy's Big Idea

Teddy Tumshie stood in the middle of Christmas Presence's town square, feeling the weight of the grey, joyless atmosphere around him. The realisation of his mistake hit him like a runaway sleigh. He had devoured the magical gingerbread house, and with it, he had gobbled up the town's Christmas spirit. But as he looked around at the gloomy faces of the townsfolk, a spark of determination ignited within him. He couldn't just stand there; he had to do something to make things right.

The first step was to enlist help. Teddy approached his best friend, Timmy Tinsel, who, despite being as thin as a string of tinsel, had a heart as big as Santa's belly. "Timmy, I need to tell you something," Teddy began, his voice shaky. He confessed everything about the gingerbread house and the magic it held. To his surprise, Timmy didn't scold him. Instead, he put a comforting hand on Teddy's shoulder.

"We'll fix this, Teddy. Together," Timmy said, his voice filled with a resolve that bolstered Teddy's spirits.

They set out to gather a team, starting with Mr. Sprinklesworth, who, upon hearing Teddy's confession, agreed to help without hesitation. Next was Mrs. Meh, formerly known as Mrs. Jingle. Her spirit seemed broken, but a flicker of hope danced in her eyes when she heard Teddy's plan to restore the town's cheer.

Together, they called a town meeting. Teddy stood in front of the community, his heart pounding. He took a deep breath and confessed his mistake to everyone. There were gasps and murmurs but also nods of understanding. Christmas Presence was a town that believed in second chances.

"We can bring back our Christmas spirit," Teddy announced, his voice gaining strength. "But I can't do it alone. We need to work together as a community."

And so, they created a plan. They would start a campaign to revive the Christmas spirit through acts of kindness, generosity, and community engagement.

The campaign started with Mr Sprinklesworth baking a giant batch of gingerbread cookies, not magical like the gingerbread house. Still, it is made with an extra dose of love and care. Mrs Meh, embracing some of her old self, helped decorate the cookies with cheerful frosting and sprinkles.

Teddy and Timmy took to the streets, handing out the cookies to passersby. At first, people were hesitant, but the sweet aroma of gingerbread was hard to resist. Slowly, smiles began to appear on the townsfolk's faces, and the square started to fill with a buzz of activity.

Next, they organised a community decorating event. The town square, which had looked so miserable, was gradually transformed. People brought out their ladders, garlands, and lights, working together to adorn every corner. Teddy, who had never lifted a finger to help, was now in the thick of it, stringing lights and hanging ornaments.

Inspired by the adults' efforts, the town's children built snowmen and painted festive scenes on shop windows. The snow, which had been grey and lifeless, now sparkled under a canopy of colourful lights.

Teddy felt something he had never experienced before— the joy of giving. He laughed and joked with people he had never spoken to, feeling part of something far bigger than himself.

Taking cue from the rising spirits, the carolers began to sing more lively tunes. Their voices, once dreary and flat, now rang out clear and strong, spreading infectious cheer. Mrs. Meh even found herself humming along, her name feeling less and less fitting with each passing moment.

As night fell, the town square was alive with a new energy. Once a sad reminder of the town's lost spirit, the Christmas tree was now ablaze with lights, the star at its top shining brightly once again.

Teddy stood back and looked around. The square was filled with laughter, music, and the sound of community— a stark contrast to the gloom that had enveloped the town just days before. He realised then that the magic of Christmas wasn't just in a gingerbread house; it was in the hearts of the people of Christmas Presence.

But their work was not done yet. The spirit was returning, but they needed something big, something truly magical, to bring back the full glory of Christmas to Christmas Presence. Teddy, with a newfound sense of purpose, knew just what to do.

Chapter 7: Sparks of Christmas Joy

In the heart of Christmas Presence, a remarkable transformation was taking place. The town, which had been shrouded in a cloak of gloom, was slowly waking up to its former glory. The change was gradual, like the first thaw of spring, but with each passing day, the festive atmosphere that had once defined the town was returning.

The once-dull fairy lights now twinkled merrily, glowing warmly on the snow-covered streets. The garlands hung limply and were now perked up, vibrant and full of life. Shop windows reflected the town's despondence and were now scenes of joy and anticipation for the holiday season.

The residents of Christmas Presence, their spirits lifted by the recent efforts, [\were actively participating in the town's revival. They adorned their homes and storefronts with extra joy, determined to make up for lost time. The sound of laughter and friendly chatter filled the air, replacing the deafening silence that had recently enveloped the town.

Teddy Tumshie, once the cause of the town's plight, was now at the forefront of its revival. Every morning, he and Timmy Tinsel would meet with Mr. Sprinklesworth and other volunteers to plan the day's activities. They organised community events, from decorating contests to festive bake-offs, each event drawing more participants than the last.

The town square, the heart of Christmas Presence, was bustling with activity. Stalls that had been empty were now filled with craftspeople selling handmade ornaments, knitted scarves, and various festive treats. The aroma of mulled wine, roasted chestnuts, and spiced gingerbread filled the air, inviting passersby to stop and savour Christmas flavours.

Children, their spirits rekindled, played in the snow, building snowmen and creating snow angels, their laughter a melody that resonated throughout the town. Once grey and lifeless, the snow now sparkled under the festive lights as if sprinkled with magic.

The carolers, their voices now full of warmth and joy, roamed the streets, spreading cheer with every note. Their songs, a mix of classic carols and cheerful tunes, became the soundtrack to the town's revival. Residents joined in, their voices harmonising in a chorus symbolising unity and shared joy.

Mrs Meh, who had tentatively begun to reclaim her title as Mrs Jingle, organised a Christmas choir. It was composed of townsfolk from all walks of life, each bringing their unique voice to the ensemble. They practised in the town square, their voices rising in a jubilant crescendo that echoed off the buildings and into the hearts of everyone who heard them.

Even the animals of Christmas Presence seemed to sense the change. The reindeer at the local farm pranced and played, their spirits lifted by the town's renewed energy. Once silent birds chirped merrily, adding their songs to the festive atmosphere.

As the days progressed, the sense of community grew stronger. Old grievances were forgotten, neighbours helped each other with decorations, and new friendships were forged. The town was restoring its Christmas spirit and building something stronger—a sense of togetherness and mutual support.

Teddy, witnessing the transformation he had helped initiate, felt a sense of pride and fulfilment he had never known. The joy of giving, of being part of something bigger than himself, was a feeling far more satisfying than any selfish indulgence he had experienced.

One evening, as Teddy walked through the town square, he looked around at the smiling faces, festive lights, and overall cheer. He realised that Christmas Presence had become more than just a town celebrating Christmas year-round. It had become a symbol of resilience, the power of community, and the magic that can happen when people come together.

However, the entire spirit of Christmas had yet to be completely restored. The grandeur and enchantment that once defined Christmas Presence were still missing. Teddy knew that to bring back the true magic of Christmas, they needed to do something extraordinary that would ignite the full brilliance of the holiday spirit in the heart of every resident.

And so, with a heart full of hope and a mind buzzing with ideas, Teddy set off to plan the grandest Christmas celebration Christmas Presence had ever seen. A celebration that would not only mark the return of the town's festive spirit but would also be a testament to the journey they had all embarked on—a journey from despair to hope, from gloom to joy, from selfishness to togetherness.

The preparations began in earnest, with everyone pitching in. The town square was transformed into a winter wonderland, with twinkling lights adorning every tree and rooftop. A massive Christmas tree was erected in the centre, taller and more magnificent than any tree the town had ever seen. It would be the centrepiece of their grand celebration, a symbol of their renewed spirit.

Local crafters crafted unique decorations, each adding their personal touch to the town's festive attire. Bakers and cooks prepared a feast that promised a culinary delight, with dishes ranging from traditional Christmas fare to exotic treats.

Teddy, Timmy, and Mr. Sprinklesworth worked tirelessly, coordinating the efforts and ensuring that every detail was perfect. They wanted this celebration to remind them of what they had all overcome and be a beacon of hope for the future.

As the day of the celebration drew near, the excitement in Christmas Presence was obvious. Invitations were sent to neighbouring towns, and the news of their grand celebration spread far and wide. People from all over the region began to arrive, drawn by the promise of a Christmas experience like no other.

The night of the celebration arrived, and the town square was a spectacle to behold. Lights twinkled like stars in a clear winter sky, the aroma of delicious food filled the air, and laughter and music created a symphony of joy. The residents of

Christmas Presence, along with their guests, gathered around, their faces reflecting the light of the grand Christmas tree.

Teddy stood in the crowd, his heart swelling with emotion. He looked at the faces around him, the children with their eyes wide with wonder, the adults with smiles of genuine happiness, and he knew they had succeeded. They had brought back the Christmas spirit to Christmas Presence.

As the clock struck midnight, the lights on the Christmas tree were lit, and the star at its top shone brighter than ever. It was a magical moment that captured the essence of Christmas—hope, joy, and the power of community.

The celebration continued into the night, singing, dancing, and merry-making. It was a night that would be remembered for years to come when Christmas Presence reclaimed its title as the town where Christmas was not just a day but a way of life.

Looking around at the happy faces, Teddy knew this was just the beginning. The true spirit of Christmas was about giving, sharing, and being together. And as long as they held on to those values, Christmas Presence would always be a place of joy and wonder.

Chapter 8: The Night Everything Changed

The evening in Christmas Presence was a vibrant tapestry of joy and celebration. The streets were alive with the sounds of laughter and music, the air tinged with the scents of festive treats and mulled wine. Having rediscovered its Christmas spirit, the town was basking in the warmth of community and joy. But amidst this backdrop of revelry, a sudden twist was about to unfold, casting a shadow over the newly rekindled cheer.

Teddy Tumshie, feeling a newfound sense of belonging and pride in his role in restoring the town's spirit, was making his way through the crowd, sharing smiles and greetings. The town square was ablaze with lights, the giant Christmas tree standing tall and proud, a beacon of the town's triumph over gloom. But as he neared the square's edge, a faint, unfamiliar smell pricked at his senses. It was subtle yet out of place amid the festive aromas—a hint of smoke.

Curious and slightly concerned, Teddy followed the scent. It grew stronger, more acrid as he wound his way through the narrow streets, away from the jubilation of the square. The merry sounds of the celebration faded into the background, replaced by an uneasy silence punctuated only by his quickening footsteps.

Turning onto Baker's Lane, the sight that met his eyes sent a jolt of shock through him. Mr Sprinklesworth's bakery, the heart of so many warm memories and sweet delights, was engulfed in flames. Bright orange tongues of fire licked at the night sky, consuming the beloved building with a fierce appetite. Smoke billowed in thick, choking clouds, painting a stark contrast against the festive lights that adorned the rest of the town.

For a moment, Teddy stood frozen, disbelief and horror gripping him. The bakery was more than just a brick and wood structure; it symbolised the town's soul, a place where warmth, laughter, and the scent of baking had blended into countless happy memories.

The fire brigade's sirens wailed in the distance, a desperate call to action that snapped Teddy out of his daze. He raced towards the bakery, his heart pounding with fear and determination. As he approached, he could see the silhouettes of people gathering, their faces illuminated by the inferno that raged before them.

Neighbours and townsfolk, drawn by the commotion, arrived in a growing throng. The contrast was jarring—the festive attire and cheerful faces now marred by expressions of shock and helplessness. The fire cast an eerie glow on their features, reflecting the weight of the moment.

Mr Sprinklesworth was there among the crowd, his usual jovial demeanour nowhere to be seen. His face was etched with anguish, illuminated by the fire's glow. The bakery was his life's work, a legacy of joy and community spirit, now being reduced to ashes and embers.

The fire brigade, a team of volunteers from the town itself, fought bravely against the blaze. Hoses were directed at the heart of the fire, trying to tame the unrelenting flames. Despite their shock, the townsfolk rallied together, aiding however they could. Buckets of water were passed along a hastily formed human chain, a collective effort to stop the disaster.

Teddy joined in, working alongside his neighbours, each bucket of water a shared expression of their determination to save a piece of their town's heart.

But as the night wore on, it became evident that the fire was winning. The old and dry bakery's structure fueled the fire, which absorbed it ruthlessly.

Despite the best efforts of the fire brigade and the townsfolk, the bakery eventually succumbed to the flames. The fire burned with a ferocity that left little hope for salvage. As the last wall collapsed, the crowd breathed a collective sigh of despair. Once a source of sweet aromas and warm welcomes, the bakery was now nothing but a smouldering ruin.

The dawn broke with a dreary light over Christmas Presence. The fire was out, leaving behind a charred skeleton of the beloved bakery. The townsfolk, their faces weary and streaked with soot, surveyed the damage in the pale morning light. A sense of loss hung heavy in the air, a strong reminder of what had been.

The tragedy of the bakery's destruction was more than the loss of a building; it was a blow to the heart of the community. It represented a shared history, a place where friendships were formed over cups of hot cocoa, and the magic of Mr. Sprinklesworth's baking had brought smiles to countless faces.

As the townspeople left, a new reality began to settle in. The challenge they faced was significant. The bakery was not just a physical space but a cornerstone of their shared experiences and memories. Rebuilding it would be a daunting task, one that would require more than just bricks and mortar. It would require the collective will and effort of the entire community.

For Teddy, standing amid the ruins of the bakery, the fire was a stark reminder how easily happiness can be taken away. But in his heart, a resolve began to take shape. The bakery had to be rebuilt, not just for Mr. Sprinklesworth but for the entire town. It symbolised their resilience and ability to rise from ashes and rebuild, stronger and more united than before.

The task ahead was daunting, but Teddy knew the spirit of Christmas Presence, community and togetherness, would see them through. The town had faced darkness before and had emerged into the light. This time would be no different.

Chapter 9: Teddy's Courageous Plan

Community collaboration was in full swing in the heart of Christmas Presence as the townsfolk, led by Teddy Tumshie, embarked on an ambitious attempt to rebuild Mr Sprinklesworth's bakery. With Christmas fast approaching, they worked urgently, determined to see the beloved bakery rise from the ashes in just a few days.

The scene was one of cheerful chaos. Neighbours who had never swung a hammer were now earnestly trying their hand at carpentry, while others, armed with paintbrushes and an array of colours, set about adding a festive touch to the building. In the thick of it all, Teddy coordinated the efforts, his voice echoing with instructions and words of encouragement.

However, the lack of professional skill soon became apparent in comical ways. On the first day, as they attempted to install the plumbing, the bakery transformed into a labyrinth of pipes that seemed to follow their own peculiar logic. When Mrs. Jingle, now Mrs. Meh, volunteered to test the newly installed sink, she turned the faucet, only to be met with the flickering of lights. Moments later, someone flipped a switch, inadvertently triggering a gush of water from the bathroom toilet, much to the amusement and surprise of everyone.

The next day brought more misadventures. To speed up the rebuild, several townsfolk tackled the electrical work. The result was a series of whimsical mishaps – opening the refrigerator caused the radio to play, and the oven seemed mysteriously connected to the doorbell. The townsfolk laughed off these quirks, their spirits undampened, putting it down to the learning curve of amateur building.

The most memorable incident occurred when Mr Sprinklesworth opened a kitchen cabinet, only to discover Mrs Meh comfortably seated on a toilet, newspaper in hand. She looked up, equally surprised, and quipped, "Well, this is one way to multitask!" The incident, bizarre and hilarious, rippled through the town. It became a light-hearted story that summarised their well-meaning but misguided efforts.

However, the mood began to shift by the second day's end. As the townsfolk stood back to survey their work, the reality of what they had undertaken settled in. The bakery, with its crooked shelves, mismatched tiles, and a maze of inexplicable wiring, was far from the professional standard they had hoped for. Their dream of restoring the bakery in time for Christmas was crumbling under the weight of their inexperience.

That evening, gathered in the town square with the bakery standing unfinished and wonky behind them, a sense of defeat began to seep through the crowd. Mr. Sprinklesworth, looking at the earnest but flawed efforts, sighed heavily. "Folks," he began, his voice tinged with affection and regret, "I think we might have bitten off more than we can chew. This bakery... it's a lost cause."

A murmur of agreement passed through the townsfolk. They had come together with the best intentions, but the task was beyond their capabilities. The realisation that they wouldn't be able to rebuild the bakery in time for Christmas was difficult to accept..

Standing amidst his disheartened neighbours, Teddy felt a deep sense of responsibility. He had led the charge, fueled by a desire to restore a piece of Christmas Presence's heart. But now, he had to accept that some tasks required skills they simply didn't possess. The bakery, a symbol of their community spirit, would not be ready to usher in the holiday season.

As they wandered away, the unfinished bakery looming in the background, the townsfolk of Christmas Presence were united in their disappointment and realisation. They had come together, facing the challenge with determination and friendships, only to be humbled by building and construction challenges.

The journey to rebuild the bakery had taken an unexpected turn, leaving them to ponder their next steps. With Christmas just around the corner, the question of how to move forward loomed large, a puzzle yet to be solved.

Teddy's resolve to make things right for his town and Mr. Sprinklesworth remained strong. The path might be unclear, but his determination to bring back the joy and spirit of Christmas Presence was as steadfast as ever.

Chapter 10: Teddy's Special Project

Christmas Eve in Christmas Presence was always magical, but it carried a bittersweet air this year. The town was quieter than usual, still feeling the sting of their failed attempt to rebuild Mr. Sprinklesworth's bakery. Teddy Tumshie, in particular, felt the weight of this disappointment deeply. He had wanted so much to bring back a piece of joy that the town had lost in the fire.

As he sat in his room, gazing out at the softly falling snow, an idea began to take shape in his mind. If he couldn't rebuild the bakery out of bricks and mortar, maybe he could create something else, something that would bring a smile to Mr. Sprinklesworth's face on Christmas Day.

Determined, Teddy headed to the kitchen, where his grandmother was preparing for the Christmas feast. "Grandma," he began, his eyes bright with excitement, "I want to make a gingerbread house for Mr. Sprinklesworth. A special one, to remind him of the bakery."

His grandmother, always supportive of Teddy's adventures, smiled warmly. "That's a wonderful idea, Teddy. Let's make it the best gingerbread house Christmas Presence has ever seen."

Together, they gathered the ingredients – flour, ginger, cinnamon, and all the other essentials. Teddy's enthusiasm was infectious, and soon, they were both immersed in measuring, mixing, and rolling out the dough.

As they cut out the walls and roof of the gingerbread house, Teddy felt his Christmas spirit rekindling. Each piece of gingerbread was a reminder of what the town had tried to accomplish.

Though they hadn't succeeded as hoped, this small act of kindness felt like a step in the right direction.

They spent hours decorating the gingerbread house, paying attention to every detail. The icing was piped on meticulously to resemble the ornate trim of the bakery, colourful candies were arranged to mimic the stained glass windows, and a tiny gingerbread baker stood proudly at the door. It was a labour of love, a tribute to Mr. Sprinklesworth and the cherished bakery that had meant so much to everyone.

As they worked, Teddy's grandmother shared stories of past Christmases, of the joys and challenges the town had faced and overcome. Teddy listened, his heart filling with a sense of belonging and history. He realised that Christmas Presence was more than just a place; it was a community of people who cared for each other through good times and bad.

Finally, the gingerbread house was complete. It stood on the kitchen table, a confectionery replica of Mr. Sprinklesworth's bakery, its sweet aroma filling the room. Teddy stood back, admiring their handiwork. It was more than just a gingerbread house; it was a symbol of hope, a reminder that even when things don't go as planned, there are still ways to spread joy and kindness.

As Teddy lay in bed that night, he felt a sense of contentment he hadn't felt in a long time. He was eager to present the gingerbread house to Mr. Sprinklesworth the following day. He hoped it would bring a smile to the baker's face and remind him that he was an essential part of the community, loved and appreciated by all.

Christmas Eve passed quietly in Christmas Presence, the town blanketed in a soft layer of snow, the twinkling lights casting a gentle glow on the streets. There was a sense of peace, a quiet anticipation of the joy and togetherness that Christmas Day would bring.

With the gingerbread house ready to be delivered, Teddy drifted off to sleep with a smile. He had learned a lot this holiday season – about resilience, community, and the importance of small gestures. He had discovered that the true spirit of Christmas lay in the heart of the community, in the bonds that connected every person in Christmas Presence.

As the clock struck midnight, signalling the arrival of Christmas Day, a sense of hope and joy quietly settled over the town. It was a hope that no matter their challenges, they would face them together with kindness, creativity, and a shared sense of purpose.

Chapter 11: The Miracle of Christmas Morning

Christmas morning dawned bright and crisp in Christmas Presence. Teddy Tumshie, usually one to dive straight into his presents, bypassed the brightly wrapped gifts under the tree this year. His mind was set on something far more important – the gingerbread house he had crafted for Mr. Sprinklesworth. He rushed to the kitchen, his heart racing, only to find the table where they had left the gingerbread house was eerily empty.

Panic setting in, Teddy dashed through the house in his pyjamas, calling out for his family. The house was silent, the usual festive buzz of Christmas morning absent. Confusion and worry mounting, he looked out the window, only to notice a gathering crowd in the centre of town, right on Baker's Lane. Wrapped in dressing gowns, nightcaps, and slippers, the townsfolk were gathering on the street, their faces a mix of wonder and excitement.

Without a second thought, Teddy threw on his slippers, grabbed his coat, and bolted out the door, the cold morning air biting at his skin. As he neared the town square, excited chatter and laughter grew louder. Turning the corner onto Baker's Lane, Teddy stopped dead in his tracks, his eyes widening in disbelief.

In the heart of the town stood a magnificent new bakery gleaming in the morning sun. It was a perfect replica of the old Sprinklesworth's Bakery, down to the most intricate details. The townsfolk, still in their nightwear, were gathered around, marvelling at the sight of the miraculously rebuilt bakery. Among them were Teddy's parents and grandmother, their faces alight with joy and surprise.

"How did this happen?" Teddy gasped, joining the crowd.

Nobody could answer. They were all as baffled as he was, their Christmas morning turned upside down by this unexpected miracle. With its warm, inviting glow, the bakery stood as a testament to something extraordinary beyond their understanding.

The door to the bakery swung open, and there stood Mr. Sprinklesworth, his usual apron replaced by a festive dressing gown. He beckoned the townsfolk inside, his eyes glistening with unshed tears. "Welcome, my dear friends, to our Christmas miracle," he announced, his voice thick with emotion.

The townsfolk filed in, their expressions a mix of awe and curiosity. Inside, the bakery was alive with fresh bread and cinnamon scents. Every detail was perfect, from the polished countertops to the gleaming ovens. It was as if unseen hands had lovingly restored the bakery overnight.

As the residents of Christmas Presence explored the bakery, savouring the warmth and the delicious aromas, laughter and chatter filled the air. Mrs. Jingle, now cheerfully reverted to her original name, tested the newly installed toilet, flushing it with a flourish to the crowd's delight. Everything worked flawlessly, the plumbing and electrics functioning as they should, starkly contrasting their previous comedic rebuilding attempts.

The atmosphere was one of joyous disbelief. They shared stories, pieced together theories about how this could have happened, and celebrated the community spirit, which may well have helped create this miracle.

As the morning unfolded, with the townsfolk still gathered in the bakery, enjoying Mr. Sprinklesworth's pastries and hot chocolate,

Teddy's gaze was drawn to the bakery window. Only then did they notice the gingerbread house sitting proudly on display, its icing glistening in the morning light. It was the perfect miniature of the bakery they were standing in, its details carefully crafted, a symbol of hope and resilience.

A hush fell over the crowd as they noticed the gingerbread house. Eyes widened in realisation and smiles spread across faces. The gingerbread house, Teddy's labour of love, had found its perfect home. It was more than just a sweet replica; it had become a symbol of their Christmas spirit, a physical embodiment of the miracle that had graced their town.

Teddy felt a fantastic sense of fulfilment amidst his friends and neighbours. The gingerbread house, a simple gesture of goodwill, had taken on a life of its own, becoming a part of the town's Christmas lore. He realised then that miracles come in many forms, sometimes as a grand, inexplicable event like the rebuilding of the bakery and sometimes as a small act of kindness that resonates with others.

The bakery was filled with joy, laughter, and community spirit as Christmas Presence celebrated. Teddy knew this was a Christmas they would all cherish forever. They had witnessed a miracle that had brought them together and reaffirmed their bonds. And at the heart of it all was a gingerbread house, a humble symbol of their enduring Christmas spirit.

Chapter 12: Teddy's Reflections

In the days following the Christmas miracle, Teddy Tumshie found himself in a reflective state. The transformation of Christmas Presence from a town touched by sadness to one blessed by a magical event really impacted him. As he walked through the snow-dusted streets, past the newly restored Sprinklesworth's Bakery, he pondered his journey, the lessons he had learned, and the true meaning of Christmas that had gradually unfolded before him.

Teddy's journey had begun as a quest to restore the town's Christmas spirit, a spirit dampened by the loss of the beloved bakery. His initial attempts, driven by a desire to fix what had been lost, were marked by the same self-centred attitude that had once defined him. The Teddy of old would have thought only of his enjoyment of Christmas, the gifts he would receive, and the treats he would devour. But the events of this Christmas had changed him.

While comedic and somewhat chaotic, the townsfolk's failed attempt to rebuild the bakery had been his first real experience of community effort. He had seen people come together, each contributing in their own way, united by a common goal. They had worked not for personal gain but for the benefit of someone they all cared about – Mr. Sprinklesworth. Though their efforts did not yield the result they had hoped for, the sense of togetherness and shared purpose was a gift in itself.

Then came the creation of the gingerbread house, a project born out of a desire to bring joy to someone else. As Teddy had mixed, rolled, and decorated the gingerbread, he had felt a growing sense of satisfaction and happiness. These emotions were new to him in this context. He had started to understand that giving, in its purest form, was about more than just exchanging presents; it was about offering a part of oneself, be it time, effort, or talent, to bring happiness to others.

The miraculous appearance of the new bakery on Christmas morning was the coming together of these lessons. It was as if the town's collective spirit, shared hopes and dreams, had manifested most extraordinarily. The joy that filled the air that day, the laughter and smiles, the sense of wonder and gratitude, were more profound and touching than any material gift could provide.

As Teddy continued his walk, he realised that the true meaning of Christmas was not found in the material parts of the holiday – the decorations, the lights, or even the gifts under the tree. It was found in the feeling – the sense of belonging, the joy of giving, the warmth of community, and the strength of unity.

With its picturesque setting and enduring Christmas spirit, Christmas Presence had always been a place of magic. But Teddy now understood that its true magic lay in its people – their ability to come together, support and care for one another, and their capacity for kindness and generosity. In its loss and miraculous restoration, the bakery had been a catalyst for this understanding.

Teddy's reflections brought him to the bakery, where he paused to look through the window at the gingerbread house on display. It was more than just a model of the building; it symbolised everything the town and he had experienced. It represented the journey from selfishness to selflessness, isolation to community, despair to hope.

Inside, Mr. Sprinklesworth was serving customers, his face alight with the joy of doing what he loved most. Teddy entered, greeted by the warm aroma of freshly baked goods and the sound of friendly chatter. The baker looked up, his eyes crinkling with a smile as he saw Teddy.

"Ah, Teddy, come in! Your gingerbread house has been the talk of the town. It's brought so much joy to everyone," Mr Sprinklesworth said, handing Teddy a warm pastry.

Teddy smiled, accepting the treat. "I'm just glad I could do something to help," he replied, thinking about how much he'd changed..

As he sat there, enjoying the pastry and the cosy atmosphere of the bakery, Teddy felt a deep sense of contentment and belonging. He had learned that the spirit of Christmas was about so much more than he had ever realised. It was about giving without expecting anything in return, being part of a community, and finding joy in the happiness of others.

The lessons Teddy had learned would stay with him long after the holiday season had passed. They had changed him, shaping him into someone better, someone who understood the value of community and the true spirit of giving. Christmas Presence, with its enduring magic and resilient spirit, had given him the greatest gift of all – the gift of growth and understanding.

As Teddy left the bakery, stepping back into the crisp winter air, he looked at his town with new eyes. Christmas Presence was more than just his home; it was a place where miracles could happen, where the spirit of Christmas was alive in every street corner, every decorated window, and in the heart of every person who called it home.

The journey he had taken and the lessons he had learned would stay with him, guiding him as he continued to grow and contribute to the community he had come to love and appreciate. Christmas

Presence had taught him the true meaning of Christmas; for that, he would always be grateful.

Chapter 13: A New Christmas Tradition

As the festive season continued after the Christmas miracle, the people of Christmas Presence found themselves amid a profound transformation. The miraculous rebuilding of Sprinklesworth's Bakery had become a symbol of hope and unity, a testament to the power of community spirit. At the heart of this transformation was Teddy Tumshie, a boy who had journeyed from self-centeredness to becoming a beacon of generosity and community spirit.

In the days following Christmas, the townsfolk, inspired by the recent events, gathered to discuss a meaningful way to remember their extraordinary experience. They wanted to establish a new tradition that would capture the essence of their renewed Christmas spirit and celebrate their unique story.

The meeting took place in the town hall, a cosy room filled with the hum of excited voices and the warmth of shared purpose. Teddy, who had become a local hero, was there, feeling a mix of pride and humility. He listened as the townsfolk shared ideas, each suggestion reflecting the joy and togetherness they had all come to cherish.

After much discussion, an agreement was reached. They would create an annual event, "The Festival of Lights and Giving," to be held each Christmas Eve. This festival would not only celebrate the miraculous return of their beloved bakery but also serve as a reminder of the importance of community, kindness, and the magic of giving.

The festival would begin with a grand illumination of the town square, where thousands of twinkling lights would be lit, symbolising the light each person brought to the community. Local crafters and children would create handcrafted lanterns in the weeks leading up to the event, each unique and representing a story or memory of Christmas Presence.

After the lighting ceremony, there would be a procession through the town, with everyone carrying lanterns. The parade would wind through the streets, a moving river of light, ending at Sprinklesworth's Bakery. There, Mr. Sprinklesworth would unveil a unique gingerbread creation, a tradition that Teddy would help to create each year.

The festival's highlight would be the "Circle of Giving," where townsfolk would gather to exchange small, handmade gifts. These gifts were not meant to be extravagant but were symbols of thoughtfulness and care. It was a time to appreciate the joy of giving and receiving, a reminder that the actual value of a gift lay in the sentiment behind it.

As the plans for the festival took shape, Teddy found himself at the centre of the preparations. He worked alongside Mr. Sprinklesworth, learning the finer points of gingerbread artistry. Together, they designed the first gingerbread centrepiece for the festival – a magnificent replica of the town square, complete with tiny lights that twinkled like stars.

The debut Festival of Lights and Giving was a complete success. As dusk fell on Christmas Eve, the town square came alive with the glow of thousands of lanterns. The air was filled with laughter and music, the scent of gingerbread and hot cocoa. Each holding a lantern, the townsfolk formed a dazzling procession illuminating the winter night.

Teddy felt a strong sense of belonging while walking alongside his family and friends. He looked around at the smiling faces, the young and the old, each person a vital thread in the fabric of their community. The sight of the lanterns, each a unique expression of creativity and personality, filled him with awe. He realised that every person in Christmas

Presence had something special to contribute, something that made the town richer and more vibrant.

At Sprinklesworth's Bakery, the crowd gathered in anticipation as Mr. Sprinklesworth and Teddy unveiled the gingerbread town square. Gasps of delight and applause filled the air as the intricate details of the creation were revealed. Teddy beamed with pride, his earlier worries replaced by the joy of accomplishment.

The Circle of Giving was heartwarming, with people exchanging gifts and stories, their faces alight with happiness. Teddy received several handmade gifts, each a token of appreciation for his role in rekindling the town's spirit. He, in turn, gave out small gingerbread figures he had made, each crafted with care and affection.

As the festival drew to a close, the townsfolk gathered around a large bonfire in the square, singing carols and sharing tales of Christmases past. The fire's warmth and the community's closeness enveloped Teddy in a feeling of contentment. He realised how far he had come since the beginning of the holiday season. He had learned the true meaning of Christmas – it was about more than just presents and decorations; it was about kindness, giving, and being there for one another.

The Festival of Lights and Giving became an annual tradition in Christmas Presence, a cherished event that brought the community together to celebrate their unique spirit. Each year, Teddy played a significant role in the festivities, transforming from a self-focused boy to a young man of generosity and community spirit, inspiring others.

As the years passed, the story of the Christmas miracle and the festival's establishment became part of the town's story. It was a story of hope, resilience, and the power of community. This story would be told for generations to come.

Teddy, once the boy who thought only of himself, had become an integral part of the town's heart and soul. He had learned that the greatest joy came from giving, being a part of something larger than oneself, and connecting with those around him.

With its twinkling lights, warm bakery, and close-knit community, Christmas Presence continued to thrive, a beacon of the Christmas spirit. And at the centre of it all was the memory of a Christmas miracle, a reminder that even in the darkest times, light and hope could be found in the hearts of people who came together with love and compassion.

The End

About The Author

Chris Duke is an author from the vibrant city of Glasgow in Scotland. From a young age, Chris was known for his imaginative storytelling, crafting tales that captivated those around him. It was at the age of 39 that Chris discovered he has ADHD and Autism, which brought clarity to his extraordinary imagination and unique perspective on the world. These traits have become integral to his storytelling, infusing his work with creativity and depth.

In his writing, Chris adopts a style that is straightforward yet engaging, akin to a friendly conversation. This approach ensures that his books are accessible and enjoyable for a wide range of readers, making complex ideas understandable and relatable.

Emotions play a central role in Chris's storytelling. He is passionate about teaching young readers that experiencing and expressing a variety of emotions is a natural part of life. Drawing from his own life experiences, Chris creates stories that resonate with children, helping them to understand and articulate their feelings.

Chris's most notable work, "Lucy's Blue Day," is a testament to his ability to connect with young minds. This picture book about emotions has not only been a favorite among readers but also a valuable resource in helping children navigate their emotional landscape.

Beyond the realm of writing, Chris harbors a keen interest in professional wrestling, an enthusiasm that adds another dimension to his creative aspirations. He dreams of one day crafting a story set in the thrilling world of wrestling.

Interacting with his readers is a source of joy and inspiration for Chris. He fondly recalls conversations with young fans, particularly a heartwarming encounter with a boy who found solace in Chris's words. These experiences are not only gratifying but also influence his approach to storytelling.

Looking forward, Chris is excited about the resurgence of "Lucy's Blue Day" in 2024. He is dedicated to reintroducing this impactful story to a new generation of readers.

Chris's advice for budding young writers is both practical and encouraging: Never leave a story unfinished. He believes in the power of perseverance, urging young authors to see their narratives through to the end, ensuring their voices are heard.

Learn more about Chris's work at

www.lucysblueday.co.uk

Printed in Great Britain
by Amazon